The Long
Journey Home

The Long Journey Home

Warren Hussey Bouton

Illustrated by Barbara Kauffmann Locke

Hither Creek Press
Laconia, New Hampshire

*This book is dedicated to
Martha, Brenda, Ben,
Sarah, Larry and the little one*

CHAPTER

1

"We're going to Nantucket!" Ben exclaimed as he bounced up and down in the backseat of our family's Jeep. Mom, Dad, Ben and I were packed in like sardines as we waited on the dock in Hyannis to catch the ferry to the island. My parents had managed to stuff suitcases, groceries, books, games, kites and our golden retriever, Sadie, into every nook and cranny. Thank goodness our bikes were tied onto the rack on the back of the car.

"I can't wait to get on the boat," Ben babbled. "First I'm going to get a hot dog at the snack bar because I'm starving! Then I'm going to

go up to the bow and count jelly fish. Sarah, do
you remember the time we were on the *Eagle* and I
counted five hundred and sixty-two jelly fish in
one trip?! That was awesome!"

"Ben, would you please calm down and make a little less noise for a while?" I muttered, "I'm trying to read."

"Oh, come on, Sarah, lighten up," my younger brother piped in. Then he screamed again at the top of his lungs, "We're going to Nantucket!"

I had to admit that I was really looking forward to our vacation on the island this year. My Dad had grown up on Nantucket and we went back just about every summer to visit my Grandma and Grandpa. Sometimes we stayed at the family cottage that was right on the beach in Madaket. Other years we settled into my grandparents' old house on Main Street where the doors squeaked, the floors creaked and it felt as if every time you walked around a corner you would run into a ghost. But no matter where we slept at night, in town or in Madaket, we always had a great time going to the beach, crabbing at Millie's bridge, biking and running errands for my grandparents around town. But this year I was happier than ever to be in a place that was familiar. Six months ago Dad had taken a new job and we had moved to a different town. Our new house was great and I had made a lot of friends at school, but I missed my old buddies. Sure, we kept in touch on the computer but it just wasn't the same and I could feel my life-long friends drifting away. Nothing was the same. That's why I couldn't wait to get to Nantucket to taste Grandma's fantastic chocolate chip cookies, to walk to the point out in Madaket, and to do all the things Ben and I had been doing since before we could remember. The only thing I hoped would be different this year was that we could relax and enjoy our vacation without meeting any ghosts! For whatever reason, it felt as if every time Ben and I visited Nantucket we managed to attract a whole variety of spooks. Some of them were friendly and others were not.

This year I needed to relax. This year all I wanted was a vacation with no ghosts.

CHAPTER

2

"What is that?" Ben yelled as a funny looking ship came around the point into Hyannis harbor.

"I have no idea," I grumbled, "but it's not the *Eagle*."

That was an understatement. The *Eagle* was huge with a big deck for cars and all kinds of space for passengers to sit, both inside and out. This boat had a wheelhouse that was way up front and behind it was nothing but a long, open deck for trucks and cars. This was not what we had expected!

"Well, unless I miss my guess," answered

Dad, "that is our ride to Nantucket. The lady at the ticket counter told me that the ferry that you like so much, the *Eagle*, broke down yesterday and is in for repairs. That means we get to ride on the beautiful freight boat known as the *Auriga*."

"The *Auriga*?" Ben questioned. "By any chance does *Auriga* mean ugly?"

"I'll be honest, it's not the most attractive ship in the world." Dad confessed. "But if it will get us to the island I think I can put up with just about anything."

"I can live with it too." I finally mumbled, "As long as I can sit outside on the deck, soak up some sun and enjoy the water, I'll be happy."

"Just make sure you put on plenty of sunscreen, Sarah," Mom insisted. "There's no sense starting off a vacation with a sunburn."

As it turned out, Mom didn't need to worry. By the time Dad backed the Jeep onto the *Auriga* with all the other cars and trucks and we managed to make our way to the few outside chairs, they were all taken. The handful of seats inside were full too, and between the babies crying and the dogs barking you'd have to be crazy to sit inside with all that racket.

Ben was still hoping that he'd at least get his hot dog, so he set out looking for the snack bar. He quickly discovered that the only food for sale on the *Auriga* was what he could find in the vending machines.

"This boat stinks," Ben grumbled as we climbed back into our Jeep for the two hour cruise to Nantucket.

"I don't understand why they won't let passengers go up into the bow," I sympathized. "If we have to ride on a freight boat they could at least let kids have a little bit of fun."

"This is stupid!" Ben fumed. "It's going to be the longest, most boring trip to Nantucket we've ever had."

Ben was right about that. But little did we know that once we arrived on Nantucket we'd be anything but bored.

CHAPTER
3

At long last, the freight boat docked in Nantucket, loaded down with its weary, bored passengers.

Driving off the boat was like driving into a carnival. There were people everywhere. Some were coming, others were going, still more were driving around in circles looking for a parking place or picking up family and friends. There were folks on bicycles pedaling across the street and people just ambling along eating ice cream cones.

"Let's drive up Main Street," I begged as we drove past Young's Bicycle Shop and approached the Whaling Museum. You really knew that you had arrived on the island when you felt the teeth chattering, bone rattling ride up Main Street's cobblestones.

As we bounced our way to Grandma and Grandpa's house Ben bubbled. "Look, there're the *Three Bricks* and here comes the monument."

"We're almost there!" I announced as we drew closer and closer. "I can't wait to sink my teeth into some of Grandma's chocolate chip cookies!"

Just as we were about to pull into my grandparents' driveway Mom gasped. "Oh my goodness! Look at what they've done to the house across the street! It's a showplace."

Last year, the house opposite Grandma and Grandpa's looked as if it was ready to fall down. The paint was peeling and some of the clapboards were rotting. The grass was never mowed and the gardens and bushes were completely overgrown. It was a disaster. But now, it was beautiful, like something out of a magazine.

"One more little change for this precious old island," Dad added as we pulled up the driveway and stopped beside Grandpa's truck.

Even before Dad had turned off the motor Ben and I burst out of the Jeep and were running for Grandma's kitchen. My mouth was watering because Grandma always seemed to know exactly when we'd arrive. Sure enough as we surged through the screen door there she was, taking a cookie sheet out of the oven.

"Well, there you are," Grandma exclaimed as she put down the hot tray and gave us a big hug.

"What are you baking Grandma?" I asked with a grin on my face and a knowing look in my eyes.

"Oh, I thought that maybe you'd like some cookies after your long trip, and just for a special treat I baked you something different...oatmeal raisin!"

Ben didn't care what kind of cookies they

were. He already had one in his mouth and two more in each hand but I was so disappointed. I had been looking forward to everything being the same. I had had enough changes in the last year and so far on this trip, everything was different. The freight boat, the house across the street, the cookies all made me wonder what was going to be next.

"Are you all right, Sarah?" Grandma asked as she passed me an oatmeal raisin cookie. Thankfully, before I had a chance to answer, Mom, Dad and Grandpa came into the kitchen carrying a few of our suitcases.

"Now who in the world is slamming screen doors around my house?" Grandpa teased, "Must be some of the neighborhood troublemakers looking for a handout. Well surprise, surprise it's Sarah and Ben munching on cookies. Some things never change!"

But after I gave Grandpa a hug and headed

out to get my backpack from the Jeep, I whispered to myself, "Some things never change…but too many things don't stay the same."

CHAPTER
4

Dinner was as lively as ever with lots of catching up. Grandpa told us about all of the work that had taken place over the winter on the house across the street and in the houses next door.

I really didn't have much to say because I was still stewing over the oatmeal raisin cookies. Besides, even if I wanted to say something I couldn't have gotten a word in edgewise because Ben just wouldn't stop talking. He went on and on about his new school, his new Little League team and the fact that he had started playing the viola.

When dinner was over Ben and Grandpa headed for the living room to renew their rivalry in checkers while Grandma, Mom, Dad and I cleared the table and started washing the dishes.

Grandma must have noticed how quiet I'd been at dinner because she asked, "Sarah, how is your new school?"

"It's okay," I mumbled.

"Oh, come on, Sarah," Mom responded. "It's more than okay. You have great teachers and a lot of new friends. The school has a wonderful music program and a drama club. You love all those things."

Hearing Mom's words I just couldn't control my feelings or my tears. "Okay, I do love all those things but it's just not the same…it's not home!"

Grandma stopped what she was doing, stooped down a little, looked into my eyes and said, "No, it's not home, Sarah. It takes time for a new place to feel right. Be patient, you'll feel at home again."

"Is it okay if I go for a walk?" I whispered as I tried to hold back the tears.

"Sure you can, honey," Mom answered. "Why don't you take Sadie and your brother with you? They've both been cooped up all day and Ben's on a sugar high from all of those cookies. Both of them could afford to burn off some energy."

"Well, there's one thing that will never change," I muttered to myself. "Somehow, I always get stuck with my annoying little brother."

CHAPTER
5

We walked down Main Street with Ben trailing behind chattering all the way and Sadie stopping every ten feet to sniff some new smell. We turned left on Gardner, then onto North Liberty and finally ambled up Woodbury to Barnabas until we came back to the top of Main Street near Caton's Circle.

"Look Sarah, the sun's starting to set," Ben noticed as the clouds in the western sky began to glow with gold, orange and red. "Let's head over to the Quaker Cemetery and watch the sky."

As we passed through the opening in the

fence it seemed hard to believe that underneath this rolling field thousands of people were buried.

As I plopped myself down on top of a little hill Sadie laid down beside me and rested her head in my lap. She could tell that I was still upset about all the changes and especially about our move.

Ben could tell too but, as always, he wasn't quite as comforting as our golden retriever. Finally, after a few precious seconds of peace and quiet he blurted, "Sarah, what's your problem?"

"What's my problem?" I bellowed. "I was all excited about coming to Nantucket because I was looking forward to getting away from all the changes in our lives. But what do I get...a boring ride on a freight boat and OATMEAL RAISIN cookies! Since when does Grandma bake oatmeal raisin cookies? I want things to be the same. I don't know who I am anymore. I don't know where home is anymore." The tears were starting to sting my eyes again. I jumped to my feet, gave a tug on Sadie's leash and declared, "The sunset's over. I'm heading back to Grandma and Grandpa's house."

When we were almost back to the fence surrounding the cemetery, I looked back at Ben and couldn't help but notice that there were three people standing right where I'd been sitting less than a minute before. They were arguing. One was a mean looking old man. He was short, round, bald and had really big evil eyes that were almost bulging from his head. He was talking angrily to a girl about my age. Standing behind the girl was a boy who could have been the same age as Ben. All three of them were wearing old-fashioned clothes. The kids kept pointing at Ben and me but the old man kept shaking his head from side to side until at last he shouted, "No, you will not!"

"Where did they come from?" Ben asked. "It's as if they appeared out of nowhere."

Then, just to be friendly, Ben called out, "Nice sunset, huh!?"

The three of them just stared at us and then without a sound they slowly faded away and were gone.

Ben and I stood there amazed and a little frightened by what we had just seen. Our spell was broken when Sadie gave the leash I was holding a pull toward Grandma and Grandpa's.

We walked in silence until I whispered at last, "Well, Ben, there's something that's the same. We're on Nantucket and we've just spotted ghosts."

CHAPTER

6

"What is all that pounding?" I shouted as I stretched and rubbed my eyes after a good night's sleep.

Last night, after our encounter in the Quaker Cemetery, it had taken me a long time to calm down and fall asleep. But once I drifted off I was dead to the world. Now, the sun was pouring through my bedroom window and so was the sound of someone hammering like crazy. Out of the blue the noise of a power saw erupted and I realized that all the racket was coming from the carpenters who were renovating the house next door.

"Why can't people just leave things alone? It's a perfectly good house," I complained to myself.

While I was still fuming, I heard Ben get out of bed and amble down the hallway to the bathroom.

Suddenly Ben called out. I could tell something was up because there was a touch of nervousness in his voice. "Sarah, you've got to come here and see this!"

"Ben, what now?" I grumbled.

"Get down here Sarah! You're not going to believe it," he whined.

I hauled myself out of bed and stomped my way to the bathroom. "What's *your* problem?" I roared.

"Look!" Ben said with astonishment as he pointed to the bathroom sink.

I could hardly believe my eyes. Right there in front of us, the water faucet was slowly turning

on and off all by itself.

"What's going on?" my little brother wondered aloud.

Staring at the faucet I started to get really angry. "I don't know for sure, but I intend to find out! Just once I'd like to come to Nantucket to relax and enjoy myself without having to deal with ghosts. So let's end the suspense here and now.

Who's there?" I demanded. "If you're a ghost show yourself."

The faucet stopped turning and right beside the sink appeared the girl and the boy that we had seen last night in the Quaker Cemetery. We just stared at each other for a minute and then, with a little bit of disbelief and a lot less anger, I asked, "Who are you and why are you here?"

Shyly the boy stepped back a little bit so that he was almost behind the girl as she seemed to collect her thoughts and said, "We don't know who we are. We need your help."

I looked Ben in the eyes, shook my head, let out a long sigh and in a low voice declared, "Carpenters hammering first thing in the morning may be a little annoying, but ghosts needing our help again is *really* annoying. Why can't we just have a normal vacation?"

CHAPTER

"Why do you need our help?" Ben quietly inquired. "Couldn't you ask the man you were with last night? Who was he anyway? He looked mean."

"He won't help us," the girl responded. "His name is Josiah Rathbone and he's very frightening. Ever since we crossed over from life to being ghosts and found ourselves in that cemetery, he's treated us like slaves. We can't remember our names and because we don't know who our family is, he thinks he can take advantage of us and treat us horribly."

"How could you forget your names, your family?" I wondered aloud.

"All we can remember is that before we died, we were both hot, as if we were burning up inside," the girl responded. "Everything was confusing. We think we might be brother and sister, but we're not even sure about that."

With that the boy, who was looking very sad added, "We must have been Quakers because of the cemetery where we were buried. If we were in any other cemetery we could look at our gravestones and find out our names. But Quakers didn't believe in them so we'll never know who we are unless you help us."

"But why us?" I blurted.

"Last night when you were in the cemetery we heard you say that you don't know who you are and that you don't know where your home is anymore. We thought that maybe you would understand how we feel and would help us. Would you help us? Please?" the girl pleaded.

"How in the world can we help you? You died ages ago and we're just here on vacation." Ben questioned.

"Could you try?" the boy begged.

I looked into the girl's eyes and understood her sadness. If I felt the way I did about moving from one town to another, losing my friends and everything that was familiar to me, I realized how she must feel.

"All you can remember is that you were hot and confused?" I asked.

"Yes, as if we had a fever," answered the girl.

I paused for a minute and then made up my mind. "Well, that's a place to start. We'll try but we can't make any promises."

And with those words Ben and I began our new spooky adventure.

CHAPTER

We made it to the dining room table just as Mom and Dad were finishing their breakfast. Grandma was scurrying around filling coffee cups and Grandpa was slipping pieces of his English muffin under the table to Sadie and his dog, Rusty.

"Well, it's about time you two showed up for breakfast," Grandma piped in. "This restaurant was almost ready to close up shop for the morning."

"Sorry," Ben answered hesitantly. "I guess we…"

"Slept in a little too long," I jumped in.

"For heaven's sake," Grandma exclaimed.

"The day's half over. Don't know how anybody could sleep the better part of the day away. Now, what would you like for breakfast? The menu for today includes waffles or pancakes. You can have strawberries or blueberries mixed in or on top. And of course there's plenty of Vermont maple syrup. What will it be?"

We quickly placed our orders and Grandma went to work. Before you could blink an eye, Ben and I were feasting on a fabulous breakfast made with tender loving care.

While Mom, Dad and Sadie moved out onto the sun porch to plan their day, Grandpa, with Rusty trotting along behind, headed off to his workshop to begin his next project and I decided it was a good time to ask Grandma, the family historian, a few questions in the hope of helping our new ghostly friends.

"Grandma, why didn't the Quakers use gravestones?"

"Where did that question come from?" Grandma wondered in surprise. "Why in the world do you want to know that?"

"We were over at the Quaker Cemetery last night watching the sunset and we were just curious." I responded.

"If I remember right," Grandma reflected, "Quakers didn't use gravestones because they believed it was like creating an idol, something to be worshipped. It's kind of amazing to think that there are thousands of people buried over there. But without gravestones it just looks like a rolling field."

"When did they start burying people there?" Ben asked.

"Well, *that* I'll have to look up," Grandma said as she started to make her way to the bookshelf in the den where she kept all her historical books on Nantucket.

"Let's see," she murmured as she checked

the index in one of the books and started flipping
through the pages. "It says here that the first
Quaker Burial Ground was out on the way to
Madaket near the south end of Maxcey's Pond.
That makes sense because the original settlement
was out that way. The cemetery you were in last

night was added in 1730 but wasn't used too much until 1760."

"Grandma," I interrupted. "Since you have that book out, was there ever a time when a lot of people got sick on the island, like with a fever?"

"You are full of questions today aren't you!" Grandma quipped. "How would I even look that up? What would be the right word to check in the index? How about sickness...no, what about diseases...no, how about epidemic...bingo! Look at that. There was a plague that hit the Indians on the island in 1763 and it sounds as if it was some kind of fever. Listen to this: 'In 1763, a *yellow fever* killed 222 out of 358 island Indians.'"

"Does it say anything about any of the settlers catching it, Grandma?" Ben asked.

"No, but that doesn't mean that they didn't," Grandma answered. "I can't imagine the folks of the time would be too keen on admitting that the Indians and the English were infected by the same illness. I'd be surprised, considering how small this island is, if it didn't hit at least a few of the settlers. Probably the elderly and children would be most likely to catch something."

The elderly and children, I thought. Maybe, just maybe, that was the clue we needed to help our mysterious young friends.

CHAPTER

9

"Kids," Mom called from the sun porch. "Your Dad and I need to do a little grocery shopping this morning. You can come with us if you want, but we thought you might like to explore downtown on your own for a while. There are probably a ton of new shops. Then this afternoon we can head off to the beach."

"Sounds like a plan, Mom," Ben piped in.

"Grandma, if we wanted to learn more about the cemetery or about the plague that hit the Indians, where would be the best place?"

"Well, aren't you two just wonderful young

students of Nantucket history!" Grandma praised. "More young people should appreciate the island the way you do. Let's see, you could go to the Nantucket Historical Association library. That's on Fair Street now. Or you could go to the town library, the Atheneum, and ask the research librarian, Louise Rounsville, where the best place to look might be. She knows more about Nantucket than just about anybody alive. You remember Mrs. Rounsville don't you? I sent you to see her once before when you were trying to learn more about that whaling ship, the *Joseph Starbuck*, that was captained by that mean, old Captain Ichabod Paddack."

Ben and I both shivered at the sound of Captain Paddack's name. We had encountered his ghost more than once while we were visiting the island and that was enough for both of us.

"I think we'll try the library," I said as Ben nodded his approval. "Mrs. Rounsville was really helpful the last time and maybe she'll steer us in the right direction again."

The two of us struck off on our quest to discover the names of our unknown girl and boy. We walked with purpose down Main Street past the Monument dedicated to soldiers from Nantucket who fought in the Civil War, past the towering elm trees, the Three Bricks and all the other big, fancy homes that line one of the most beautiful streets in the world. We took a left at the newspaper store known to everyone as The Hub and soon found ourselves standing in front of the Nantucket Atheneum. It was a huge white building with massive columns that made me feel very small. We just hoped that somewhere inside that great, big library we'd find the answer that we needed.

CHAPTER
10

Ben and I bounded up the stairs past the gigantic columns, turned left at the amazing display of scrimshaw and found the circulation desk. Our hearts sank at first, when we didn't see Mrs. Rounsville's pleasant face behind the desk, but then with a shuffle and a quiet, "Hello, children," she suddenly appeared from between the bookshelves adding, "Is there something I can help you with today?"

"Hi, Mrs. Rounsville," I said quickly. "We're interested in some Nantucket history and our Grandmother suggested that we talk to you. We were wondering if there might be a way to find out the names of the people buried in the Quaker Cemetery."

Mrs. Rounsville cocked her eyebrow and pursed her lips while she thought. Finally she said, "Hmm, that's an interesting question. I'm not sure we have any books or records that would list the names of those buried there, and of course the orthodox Quakers didn't use gravestones. The few stones that are in the cemetery are from two later offshoots of Quakerism. But let me think...you might be better off going to the Historical Association Library but then...I've got just the thing. No need to trundle off to the Historical Association. Come with me."

From the circulation desk we headed back toward the front of the building up a spiral staircase to a door marked "computer room." In we went as Mrs. Rounsville announced, "Now, technically you need to have a library card to use one of these computers but since you're with me and doing research, I think we can make an exception."

Mrs. Rounsville plopped us down at a table with a laptop computer and said, "First, you need to go to nha.org. That's the Nantucket Historical Association website. Once there you'll find that it has two projects online that might help you. One is a genealogical database that lists countless names, birth dates, dates of death, marriages, parents and children. The other is their Cemetery Project. They have gathered as much information as possible about all the cemeteries on the island, including maps, names of those buried, pictures of gravestones, which, in the case of the Quaker Cemetery, won't really help you. But if you know the date of death, you might be able to do a search and see what, or rather who, comes up. It's worth a try anyway. I'll leave the two of you to your research and if you need any more help you just come and find me."

"For a little, old lady she's pretty smart about computers." Ben whispered as Mrs. Rounsville shuffled off through the door and down the stairs.

"Let's try the Cemetery Project," I said softly as I clicked on the computer link. The screen shifted and there was the opening page to a database. We could select the cemetery and then search by name or date of death.

"This should be easy," said Ben. "If they caught the same fever that hit the Indians, we know that they died in 1763. It's simple."

"Don't count your chickens before they hatch." I muttered. Something told me that nothing about this search was going to be easy.

CHAPTER
11

With a nervous sigh I entered "1763" into the date of death block on the screen and then hit the search button. The screen blinked. A page with the simple word "searching" appeared and then the screen changed again. A list of people who had been buried in the Quaker Cemetery in 1763 came into view.

"I told you this was easy," Ben yelped a little too loudly for a library.

The list included the last names, first names, their ages when they died and their date of death. There were a lot of them.

We scanned the list one name at a time.

Everybody was older than our young, spooky friends until we came to the very end and there was a list of five children with just first names: "Rebecca, age 12; Hezekiah, age 11; Phoebe, age 11; Nathaniel, age 8; Jonathan; age 7."

"What good is that?" Ben complained. "They could be any of them! Why don't they have any of the last names?"

"I don't know! Maybe it's because the loss of a child was so sad to the whole community that they all felt the pain, not just one family. Who knows? We have to work with what we've got. I think we can eliminate Hezekiah," I said hesitantly. "I'm pretty sure that's a boy's name and according to his age, he'd be too old for the boy we met. So it's Rebecca or Phoebe, Nathaniel or Jonathan."

"Maybe we could go to the other online database and search that one to find the last names," Ben wondered aloud.

"That would take forever, Ben," I answered. "We'd be here for our whole vacation. There are like a hundred thousand Nantucket names in that thing. We've got four first names which is more than we had when we walked in here. Maybe if we tell our friends the possibilities, they'll remember their own names. If not, we'll have to come up with another idea. It's almost time for lunch. How about we head back to Grandma and Grandpa's, think about it at the beach and then try to find the kids at sunset?"

"Sounds like a plan to me," Ben responded.

As we stepped out of the library and stood between the enormous columns, it was clear something was happening. The weather had been bright and beautiful when we'd gone into the Atheneum but now the clouds were dark and threatening. Suddenly there was a bolt of lightning and the wind started to whip. Everybody around us started to run for cover but Ben and I were glued to

our places because there in front of us stood the very angry, haunting presence of Josiah Rathbone, the other ghost from the cemetery. He stared at us through blazing red eyes and snarled with a booming voice that sounded like thunder, "Mind your own business and stay away from my young slaves. They…don't…need…your…help! Get in my way and you'll end up haunting the cemetery yourselves and you'll NEVER find your way home."

Out of the blue there was another terrific bolt of lightning and a horrifying crack of thunder…and he was gone. The sun broke through the clouds and it was as if nothing had even happened.

Ben and I looked at each other and with dread in my voice I said, "Ben, something tells me that Josiah Rathbone is going to be a problem."

CHAPTER
12

Ben and I slowly, quietly, and thoughtfully made our way back to Grandma and Grandpa's house and were met with enough food for lunch to feed an army. Grandma had the table spread with plates of seafood salad, chicken salad, cold cuts, rolls, bread, deviled eggs, and a huge bowl of Cape Cod Potato Chips.

"Now, what would you like to drink?" Grandma asked. "I've got lemonade, iced tea, milk, ginger ale, water and don't forget to leave room for some oatmeal raisin cookies!"

I rolled my eyes at the mention of the cookies but thankfully Grandma didn't see me.

When lunch was almost over Mom announced, "Once you clear the table, you both need to scoot upstairs and get ready for the beach. Dad and I decided we'll go to the Jetties today and save Madaket for tomorrow."

Madaket was my favorite beach but I really liked going to the Jetties. It was always fun watching the boats on their way in and out of the harbor. You could spend all kinds of time watching people learning to windsurf and counting the number of times they fell off the board into the water. It was also a good place for Ben and me to go for a walk, talk about our encounter with Josiah Rathbone and figure out what in the world we were going to do next to help our ghostly friends.

With the table cleared and the Jeep packed with all of our gear for the beach, we headed off to an afternoon of sun and sand. Dad was lucky to find a parking space right away and we hauled all of our stuff to a perfect spot not far from the water and the playground.

"There goes another one," Ben commented as one more novice windsurfer took a tumble into the water.

"Ben, how about we walk down to the rocks and see if we can spot the fast ferry on her way in." I suggested.

When we were far enough away from my parents' ears I asked, "What are we going to do now? That Rathbone guy is scary!"

"Yeah, and he looked pretty angry, too," Ben added. "I don't think I want to haunt the Quaker Cemetery forever."

"No kidding," I responded. "I thought I felt confused and lost *before* I came to Nantucket. I don't think I could stand *never* finding home."

"But look," Ben said. "We've faced a lot of scary ghosts here before and we never got hurt. Captain Paddack was pretty terrifying but we survived. That ghost that was haunting the house across the street and bullied Oliver was really mean and nasty but we came out of that okay. What's one more creepy spook? He's probably nothing but a windbag."

"I don't know, Ben. Those red eyes kind of got to me," I answered as we stopped walking and sat down on the rocks of the jetty.

"Sarah, let's not worry about Rathbone. How about we try to solve the problem of finding out who those kids are. If we're scared of Rathbone, think about how they must feel. We might be the only chance for them to be free of him." Then my little brother added, "I've been thinking. We got as much information as we could from that database online. We've got four possible first names, but no last name. What we need to find is someone who lived closer to 1763."

"Ben, everybody who lived anywhere close to 1763 is long gone," I whispered with an exasperated tone to my voice.

"Exactly," Ben replied. "But do you remember Cyrus and Abigail, the ghosts we helped when we went through the cellar door and found ourselves going back in time?"

I remembered all right. We had saved Abigail from the Great Fire of Nantucket. Cyrus' ghost had led us through Grandma and Grandpa's cellar door and somehow we had found ourselves back in 1853. Ben had nearly been turned to toast when a burning elm tree fell. But in the end we were okay and Abigail and Cyrus had ended up getting married.

"But Ben, 1853 is ninety years after the fever struck the island," I argued.

"I know," Ben responded. "But if the fever was such a big deal somebody is bound to remember something, especially if it killed five kids! What have we got to lose?"

"Well, besides the threat of haunting a cemetery forever," I gulped. "I guess...nothing.

But how are we going to talk to Cyrus and Abigail?"

Ben smiled, "Don't worry. I have a brilliant idea."

CHAPTER
13

The rest of the afternoon at the beach was fantastic. We splashed. We dove. We chased after a Frisbee and we flew our kite. It was a great day, and for a while everything felt normal again. I forgot about moving and losing my old friends. I didn't even think about the two young ghosts from the Quaker Cemetery and thankfully I was even able to forget about the ghost of Josiah Rathbone for a while.

The afternoon flew by and Dad finally announced that we needed to call it a day. By the time we got back to the house, Grandma had another feast on the table. I have no idea how one woman could possibly produce so much food for every meal. "Grandma just likes to cook," Mom would always say. And as far as I could see that was an understatement! Tonight it was pork chops with tomato sauce and lots of onions. There was a mountain of the best garlic bread you ever tasted and more salad than Ben and I would ever eat, especially since Ben never touched anything that was green. We laughed, we talked, Grandpa teased, Ben rolled his eyes every time Grandpa said he couldn't remember our names. It was just like old times.

As we were clearing the table I whispered to Ben, "How about we take a walk to the cemetery and see if our friends can remember anything else."

He nodded and before Mom or Grandma could rope us into helping with the dishes, we snuck out the kitchen door.

We approached the opening in the fence to

the Quaker Cemetery and as soon as we set foot on that sacred ground, the clouds above us started to swirl. The sky became gray and the wind began to blow.

"I think we're going to have a problem." I mumbled with just a little bit of fear in my voice.

Ben and I kept walking even as thunder cracked in the distance.

"How are we going to find them?" Ben wondered aloud.

"Let's go to the spot where we first saw them and maybe they'll show themselves," I answered. "Beyond that I have no idea."

We reached the place where the ghosts had appeared before and waited...and waited...and waited. We called out the names we had discovered, "Rebecca...Phoebe...Nathaniel... Jonathan."

The clouds became darker and angrier. There was a lightning strike at the corner of the cemetery and the wind gusted through the tall grass and bushes. No one came. But in the wind we heard the horrible voice of Josiah Rathbone whispering, "Go away," over and over.

Finally, there was a huge clap of thunder right over our heads and we ran as hard as we could to the opening in the fence. As we burst through the gate, the wind stopped and the sky cleared.

"Josiah Rathbone is not a very pleasant ghost," Ben murmured.

"That's for sure," I agreed. "It looks like we move to plan B. Are you ready to tell me your brilliant idea now?"

CHAPTER
14

As we headed off to bed that night Ben revealed his brilliant idea. We decided that we would wake up well before breakfast and try going through the cellar door to find our way back to Cyrus and Abigail and 1853. We didn't know if it would work but we felt as if it was worth a try.

As soon as the dawn's early light came through my window the next morning, I was up, out of bed, dressed and shaking Ben awake.

"Do we have to do this today?" Ben groaned as I pulled off his covers and threatened to tickle his feet if he didn't start moving soon.

"It's now or never little brother. Those two kids need to be free from Rathbone and the sooner the better," I said in a low voice hoping that I wouldn't wake my parents or Grandma and Grandpa.

We tiptoed down the stairs to the front hall and then opened the door to the cellar. The stairs to the cellar creaked as we snuck down and once our feet touched the floor, there ahead of us was another door. It looked ordinary enough, and to most people it was just the door from the cellar outside to the driveway. But several summers ago we had discovered something magical or at least haunted about that door. That summer, when Ben and I visited Grandma and Grandpa, we had encountered another ghost, Cyrus, who had needed our help. He had led us into this very same cellar and when we went through that door we had found ourselves back in 1853. And now, to help the kids in the cemetery, we were hoping to do it again.

I walked up to the door, unlatched it and pushed it open. Everything looked normal outside. I could see the streetlight on the electrical pole across the street and then a car drove by.

"Maybe it doesn't work anymore," I wondered aloud as I walked through the doorframe with no results. Going back into the cellar I declared, "I don't think this is going to work, Ben. Nothing happened."

"How about we go through together. I'm pretty sure that's how we did it before," Ben remembered as he took my hand.

"Let's think about Cyrus and Abigail and those two kids in the cemetery and how much they need our help as we go through. Then, maybe it'll work," I said in a low, nervous voice. "On the count of three, we go! One…two…three!"

Ben and I jumped through the doorframe hand in hand. There was a brilliant flash of light and as we looked at each other standing in the

driveway we knew immediately that we had found our way back in time. Ben's t-shirt, shorts and sneakers had been transformed into a long sleeved shirt that billowed out around his wrists, knickers, long stockings and shoes with brass buckles. My outfit had changed too! I was wearing a long dress with a frilly apron and of all things, a bonnet.

"Well, it looks as if we've found our way back to 1853," I said as a horse and buggy trotted by. "Let's try to find Cyrus and Abigail as fast as we can because Grandma won't be happy if we're not at the table in time for breakfast!"

CHAPTER

15

"Now that we're here, what do we do?" Ben asked. "Maybe we should have thought this through a little more before we did it."

"It's simple, Ben," I said as I grabbed his arm and headed for the front door of what would one day be Grandma and Grandpa's house. "The last time we saw Abigail she was here with Cyrus' parents. We know he came back from a whaling trip and they were married. My guess is that if we knock on this door we'll find them."

Climbing up the front steps I took a deep breath as I knocked on the door as loudly as I could.

"Isn't it a little early to be knocking on doors?" Ben wondered out loud.

"I sure hope not because at this point we're committed." I said as we heard the locks unfasten. The door opened slowly and there standing before us was a huge man that we recognized as Cyrus' father.

"May I help you young lady?" the man asked suspiciously. "Do I know you? You look a bit familiar."

"We're old friends of Cyrus and Abigail," I answered hesitantly. "We were…away for awhile and just returned…recently. Is either Abigail or Cyrus here? We'd love to see them."

"Cyrus is off to sea again," the man said still looking at us with curiosity. "Abigail has gone to the market. She should be home shortly. Would you like to come in and wait a while? I could swear I recognize you from someplace. Please come in. Maybe if I ask you some questions we could figure out how I know you."

"No!" I responded quickly. "We'll just go to the market too and try to find Abigail there. Thank you for your help."

Ben and I scampered down the stairs and headed toward town.

"Why didn't we just wait there for Abigail?" Ben asked. "He seemed nice enough and it would save us a lot of walking."

I shook my head and said, "Ben, he was going to ask too many questions and before you know it, we'd be in trouble up to our eyeballs. It's better we find Abigail on our own."

As we walked to town it was incredible how much the streets looked the same. Sure there weren't any parked cars, overhead streetlights, telephone poles or power lines but seeing the familiar old houses made us feel right at home. As we approached the downtown it was clear that the rebuilding after the Great Fire was well underway.

Construction was going on everywhere. The carpenters and bricklayers were well into their hard day of work.

Beyond the construction we could see the masts of whaling ships tied up at the docks and anchored in the harbor. There was activity everywhere and we became so interested in everything that was going on around us that we almost forgot we were looking for Abigail until we spotted her carrying a large open basket filled with things from the market.

"Abigail!" I shouted as Ben and I ran to greet her.

"Sarah and Benjamin! What a surprise to see you again! You just disappeared after you saved me from the fire and I never had a chance to thank you."

I thought as quickly as I could and said, "We're sorry about that Abigail, but...we had other places to go and other things to do. And sadly we don't have a lot of time now either. We're trying to help some friends who need to learn about their family history here on the island. Could you try to answer a few questions for us?"

"I could try," Abigail answered. "But Cyrus is better at remembering things like that than I am. It's too bad he's away at sea. Of course, you could ask his father."

"No!" Ben jumped in. "I'm sure he could be very helpful but we feel more comfortable talking to you."

"He can be a bit intimidating at times. He always has so many questions," Abigail admitted.

"Well, here's a question for you, Abigail," I said. "Do you remember ever hearing about a sister and a brother who died about ninety years ago from a horrible fever? We think the girl was named Rebecca or Phoebe and the boy was Nathaniel or Jonathan."

Abigail thought for a long minute. "I do

remember hearing tales of something like that. It was very sad for the whole community. But I'm sorry. I can't possibly remember any names."

I was so upset. We had taken a huge risk traveling back in time in the hope of finding the names of our ghostly friends. But it was all for nothing.

"Did you ever hear of a man named Josiah Rathbone?" Ben piped up.

"I've heard stories about him!" Abigail responded. "He was a scoundrel, a very dangerous man. He may have professed to be a Quaker but the tales that are told about him speak of a dark, evil soul."

"Great...just great!" I moaned. "That's one bit of history I didn't want to hear."

CHAPTER
16

The flash of light blinded me as Ben and I joined hands and went through the cellar door returning to our own time.

"What are we going to do now?" Ben asked.

"We'd better get upstairs quick or Grandma won't give us any breakfast!" I answered as I started to run for the dining room table.

"Where have you two been?" Grandma scolded. "Have you been down in that dusty, smelly old cellar again? I don't know what in the world the attraction is down there except that with all the cobwebs it's pretty spooky. What a way to start out a beautiful day down there with the spiders and creepy crawlies. But let's keep this kitchen moving. Today we've got eggs. You can have them scrambled, fried, as an omelet or soft boiled on toast. Your parents went for Spanish omelets, that's with peppers, onions and a little salsa on the side but that might not suit your taste buds."

Ben and I both settled on scrambled eggs and by the time Grandma sat down beside us there was a pile of toast, muffins, and donuts in front of us too.

"Your Mom and Dad were up early and are off this morning to see an old friend in 'Sconset," Grandma informed us, "and Grandpa is off having coffee with some of the men he used to work with before he retired. So here we are. Your Mom said you might go to the beach in Madaket this afternoon but what do you two have planned for the morning?"

"We're not really sure, Grandma," I

responded slowly. "You know we've been learning about the Quaker Cemetery and the fever that hit the Indians. Well we think some of the settlers' children might have died of the fever too. We've found four first names: Rebecca, Phoebe, Nathaniel and Jonathan. We haven't been able to find any last names. We've tried and tried to discover who they were but we're at a dead end. It's really important to us and we just don't know where else to turn."

"Hmm, I'm not sure if you'll be able to solve this one." Grandma murmured as she thought out loud. "Was Mrs. Rounsville able to help you at the library?"

"She helped us find the first names," Ben offered. "But that's as far as we got."

"It's too bad old Hannah Hussey isn't still around," Grandma said wistfully. "She knew more about the history of this island and the people who lived here than anyone, even Mrs. Rounsville. But she's been gone for years and years."

Ben and I looked at each other with a flash of excitement. "Hannah Hussey?" I questioned. "Is that the Hannah Hussey who lived in a fishing shack out in Madaket?"

"Yes, that's the one. But how do you know about her? Like I said, she's been gone for years."

By the time Grandma's last words were out of her mouth, Ben and I were out the kitchen door and rushing for our bikes.

"We're not waiting for Mom and Dad, Grandma," I called out as we pedaled down the driveway. "We're riding our bikes to Madaket, NOW!"

Ben and I had a new lead to follow and it would mean tracking down another of our old, ghostly friends, Hannah Hussey.

We had met Hannah when Mom, Dad, Ben and I were staying at the family cottage in Madaket. Our golden retriever, Sadie, had run off while chasing seagulls and when Ben and I finally found her she was sitting in front of a tall thin, funny looking woman wearing an old-fashioned dress who stood ramrod straight and didn't mince any words. The ancient fishing shack that she seemed to live in was up a long path in the beach grass and hidden away in the sand dunes. At first we didn't realize that she was a ghost but after she helped pull our rowboat out of a fierce current that would have taken us out to sea, Hannah just faded away before our eyes as she walked up the beach. It was then that we knew Hannah Hussey was a ghost. She was friendly, as much as a stern old native of Nantucket could be, but she was a ghost with answers and now we had to find her.

CHAPTER

17

Ben and I pedaled our bikes past Maxcey's Pond, the Nantucket Landfill and Recycling Center, over the first bridge and the second bridge and at long last made it to the beach at the end of Madaket Road. It would have been easier to leave our bikes at the family cottage but much to our disappointment this year someone was renting it so we found a bike rack at the beach and locked them up.

As soon as our toes touched the sand and we looked down toward the point, I couldn't believe my eyes.

"The beach has changed so much," I exclaimed. "It looks as if half of it has been washed away!"

I knew that the ocean currents off Madaket were bad but I never expected to see the beach so narrow.

Walking along, Ben and I were amazed to discover how close the water was to some of the houses and then we spotted the biggest surprise of all.

"Look, Sarah!" Ben shouted. "The ocean cut through a low spot in the sand dunes and there's an opening right into Madaket Harbor. There's a new point! We can't walk way out to the end and look over to that other island anymore."

"Wow, now there's a new island," I added.

As we drew closer to the new point there were signs stuck into the sand warning everybody that it was too dangerous to swim. But you really didn't need to read a sign to see that you shouldn't even put a foot into the water. The sand dropped off quickly from the beach and the currents were ripping through the new channel so fast that waves were breaking over waves. A seagull in the water floated by so fast I almost thought it had an outboard motor under its feathers.

"Chalk up another change for the island," I muttered as I shook my head.

"Yeah, but not everything has changed," Ben said as we rounded the point and headed down the beach along the edge of Madaket harbor. "Look there! Isn't that the path to Hannah's shack?"

"It sure is, Ben!" I said as I began to run between the dunes. "Let's see if she has something important to tell us so that we can solve this little mystery and save our friends from that mean, old spook, Josiah Rathbone."

CHAPTER
18

Rounding a curve in the path Ben and I spotted Hannah's little fishing shack. The gray shingled walls were covered in weathered buoys. There was a huge pile of stinky, old scallop shells right beside the front door and next to them lay a pair of antique oars and worn out fishing nets.

Even though we knew Hannah was a friendly ghost, Ben and I both got a case of the tingly nerves as we approached the door that was covered with cobwebs.

"I know Hannah saved us once before," Ben whispered as we peeked into the shack, "do you think she'll be happy to see us?"

Suddenly a voice erupted behind us causing Ben and me to just about jump out of our skin. "And what might you children be doing here?"

Turning quickly we spotted Hannah Hussey who was standing right in back of us with her

hands on her hips. She had just appeared out of nowhere and there she was with her thin face, long nose and her hair pulled back into a bun.

"Do you always walk onto someone's property unannounced and then just prance into someone's home?" Hannah bellowed, "Or do you save that honor just for me?"

"We're sorry," I answered, looking down at the sand between my toes as I spoke. "We came to see you because we need your help."

"That seems to be a habit for the two of you," Hannah sputtered. "Why should I help you again?"

With that, Ben jumped in, "It's not really us that need the help. There's a girl and a boy, who we met in the Quaker Cemetery. They're ghosts...too. As far as we can find out they died in 1763 from the fever that hit the Indians on the island."

"When they caught the fever," I added,

"they became confused and lost their memory. When they died and became ghosts they couldn't remember their names or anything."

Ben was starting to get excited and blurted out, "Then a mean, old ghost named Josiah Rathbone started to take advantage of them. He treats them like slaves and the only way they can get away from him is to find out who they are."

"Josiah Rathbone, you say..." Hannah murmured as she narrowed her eyes and slowly shook her head. "Do you have any idea what the names of these children might be?"

"We've narrowed it down to Rebecca or Phoebe for the girl," I responded. "And we think it's either Nathaniel or Jonathan for the boy. We're pretty sure that the ghosts we met were sister and brother. Our grandmother said if anybody on the island would have known the answer it would have been you...but since you died years ago she couldn't think of anybody else that could help."

A small grin started to appear on Hannah's face, "Gone, but not forgotten. Well, the good news is that I may not be quite the same as I used to be, but I'm still around. Come with me."

Hannah marched past us into her little shack and started rummaging around on an ancient table tucked into the corner. It was stacked with old books and dust was flying everywhere as she dug through the pile. Pulling out a collection of brittle papers, Hannah scanned them quickly and announced as she tapped the side of her head, "The answer was right here inside my head but this is too important to leave just to my sometimes faded memory. Only one sister and brother caught the fever and died and they were, indeed, Phoebe and Nathaniel." Hannah then paused and added slowly, "Their last name was the same as mine…Hussey. I think it's time to end Josiah Rathbone's fun and set those children free."

CHAPTER 19

We stood at the gate to Quaker Cemetery as the storm clouds gathered, the wind began to whip and thunder started to crack in the distance.

Ben and I had ridden our bikes as fast as we could from Madaket and had arrived at the cemetery out of breath but determined to help our ghostly friends.

I took a step into the graveyard and a horrible rumble of thunder crashed right over our heads. Rain started to pour and there, standing right in front of us, was Josiah Rathbone with Phoebe and Nathaniel cowering behind him.

Rathbone's eyes flared red as he screamed over the sound of the wind and the rain, "Leave this place! Take even one more step and you will be doomed to walk this cemetery forever! Set them free and YOU will be my slaves!"

Ben and I were both soaked to the bone and shivering in the rain. We were terrified and took a step back. The wind began to roar even louder in our ears and lightning seemed to strike all around us. How could we possibly face this terrifying ghost by ourselves?

My heart sank, but I couldn't imagine walking that cemetery forever, "We can't do it, Ben," I cried as we hugged each other and looked into the eyes of Phoebe and Nathaniel.

We started to turn away and then heard the booming voice of Hannah Hussey as she marched right by us and surged into the cemetery, "Josiah Rathbone, you old windbag! You always were a bully. Stop your foolishness this minute and let those children go!"

With Hannah's words, Rathbone's eyes went wide, the wind and the rain stopped, the clouds started to clear and he began to stutter, "Ha-Ha-Hannah Huh-Huh-Hussey, I thought you were haunting out in Mad-Mad-Madaket!"

"Yes, and I'm sure that's where you'd like me to stay. I am partial to Madaket but when I find out that a bully is picking on my family, that's where I need to be." Hannah barked. "You've known all along who those children are. They're my kin and you've terrorized them long enough. Get away from them NOW!"

And in a blink of an eye, Josiah Rathbone was gone.

"Children, come here," Hannah said to our ghostly young friends. "Sarah and Ben have something to tell you."

CHAPTER
20

Together, Ben and I stepped up and held out our hands and our two, spooky friends laid their hands on ours. It wasn't like holding real hands but I could feel something as if a feather had brushed my skin. I smiled and said gently, "Your name is Phoebe...Phoebe Hussey." Her eyes blinked and a ghostly tear began to streak her cheek.

Then Ben looked at the boy and whispered, "You're Phoebe's brother, Nathaniel...Nathaniel Hussey and you don't have to worry about Josiah Rathbone anymore."

"Yippee!" Nathaniel shouted as the sound of his voice echoed over the hills of the Quaker Cemetery.

We stood there for a moment as the sun began to set in the west over Madaket and slowly, one by one, more ghosts began to appear and surround Phoebe and Nathaniel. There were smiles and hugs as the Hussey family was reunited.

As the ghosts gathered, I backed away to the edge of the cemetery and sat down next to a beach plum bush and began to cry. While we were searching for Phoebe and Nathaniel's names, I had almost forgotten my own sadness about my family's move, losing my friends and not knowing where home was anymore, but now that I could see the happiness of our ghostly friends, it all came flooding back.

The tears fell and I felt empty, not knowing where to turn or what to do. As I wiped my cheeks I realized that I wasn't alone. I looked up and there was Hannah Hussey. "Child, aren't you happy for Phoebe and Nathaniel?"

"I am," I mumbled through my tears, "but I'm sad for myself. Everything has changed for me since we moved and I just don't know who I am anymore or where my home is."

"Sarah, look around you." Hannah said with a gentleness I'd never heard from her before. "Precious child, do you see Phoebe and Nathaniel? They're your ancestors. They're Husseys. Cyrus and Abigail are Husseys. Your grandmother and your father are Husseys. You and Benjamin are Husseys. Our family has been a part of this island since the first English settlers felt its' sand under their feet. Our roots on this island are your roots. Wherever you might be, you will always be a Hussey and Nantucket will always be your home."

It felt as if a weight had been lifted from my shoulders. I jumped up, spun around with my arms held high and shouted at the top of my lungs,

"Nantucket's my home! It will always be my home!"

I grabbed Ben's hands and swung him around until we finally collapsed in a heap and it was then that we heard a familiar voice calling to us.

"Well, there you are! Don't you know it's past your dinner time? And just look at you. You're soaked to the skin." Grandma shouted as she walked into the cemetery. "I don't know why but I had a feeling you might be over here. Now you get back to the house. Grandpa was fussing so much about being hungry that I finally fed him and your parents but I've been keeping your dinner warm. I also made you a special surprise for dessert."

"A surprise for dessert?" Ben questioned as we scampered toward the cemetery gate. "What kind of surprise?"

"If I told you, it wouldn't be a surprise," Grandma answered. "But they're made with chocolate chips!"

"Chocolate chip cookies!" I shouted. "Now I know I'm home! I'm home for good!"